The DEADLY SECRET of ROOM 213

by Dee Phillips

illustrated by Anthony Resto

BEARPORT
PUBLISHING

New York, New York

Credits

Cover, © Fer Gregory/Shutterstock, © Fresnel/Shutterstock, © Katrina Elena/
Shutterstock, and © NAAN/Shutterstock.

Publisher: Kenn Goin
Editor: Jessica Rudolph
Creative Director: Spencer Brinker

Library of Congress Cataloging-in-Publication Data in process at time of publication (2017)
Library of Congress Control Number: 2016020330
ISBN-13: 978-1-944102-32-6 (library binding)

For more information, write to Bearport Publishing Company, Inc.,
45 West 21st Street, Suite 3B, New York, New York 10010.
Printed in the United States of America.

10 9 8 7 6 5 4 3 2 1

Contents

CHAPTER 1

The Retreat Hotel

Josh dragged his suitcase into the lobby of the Retreat Hotel.

His dad followed behind, carrying lots of tools. "This is our home for the summer, kiddo!" he said.

Josh stared at the peeling paint and **antique** furniture in the big, **dilapidated** hotel. A sign that said CHECK IN hung on a rusty chain above an **ornate** wooden desk. Josh marched up to the desk and hit a small brass bell. *Ding! Ding! Ding!*

"What do you want?" a voice snarled.

Suddenly, Josh was face-to-face with a short wrinkled man who had popped up from behind the desk.

"Uh, hi," said Josh's dad. "You must be Reggie Baker. The owners of the hotel tell me you used to work here as a **bellhop**, and you stayed to keep watch over the place after it

was closed down."

Ignoring Dad, the man pulled a cloth from his pocket and began polishing the brass bell.

Josh stared at the grumpy little man. He guessed that Reggie had to be at least eighty years old. Wisps of white hair sprouted from under the man's red cap, and he wore a faded red jacket with rows of buttons.

Dad tried again. "My name is Ben Silva. This is my son, Josh. I'm the new repairman, and I'm here to fix up the hotel before it reopens later this year."

"I was expecting you," growled Reggie. He shuffled from behind the desk. "I'll show you to your apartment."

Josh and his dad followed Reggie through a door marked STAFF ONLY and down a corridor. Reggie stopped in front of one of the doors in the hallway and handed a key to Dad.

"This is where you'll live," said Reggie gruffly. "Let's get one thing straight. You stay out of my way, and I'll stay out of yours." Then he walked away.

Josh's heart sank. Now that he'd met the hotel's only other resident, he was less excited about living at the Retreat.

As they started unpacking their suitcases, Josh asked his dad, "How old is this place?"

"It's almost one hundred years old," said Dad. "It was a popular vacation spot for rich people and movie stars. But over the years, fewer people came, so the owners closed it down."

"Can I take a look around the hotel?" asked Josh.

Dad nodded. "But be back for dinner in an hour, and don't bother old Reggie. He doesn't seem to like company."

Josh made his way back to the lobby. He spotted a large glass cabinet that contained faded black-and-white photographs of the actor Charlie Chaplin, the gangster Al Capone, and other famous visitors to the hotel.

As he studied the pictures, Josh was sure he saw one of them move! He jumped when a gray rat appeared from behind a photograph of the hotel. The creature gnawed on the photo's wooden frame. Then the rat eyed Josh and quickly disappeared to the back of the dusty cabinet.

THE RETREAT HOTEL 1935

Josh hurried across the lobby toward a pair of large glass doors. The word BALLROOM was **etched** into the glass. Josh pushed open the doors and stepped inside.

Moonlight streamed in through the ballroom's windows. Josh noticed a gaping hole in the high ceiling and large pieces of smashed plaster on the wooden floor.

Fwap, fwap, fwap. Josh heard a flapping noise. On the wall, he saw the shadow of a giant winged creature. Josh froze in terror.

Whoosh! A small bat whizzed past Josh's cheek and darted around the ballroom. In the moonlight, the little animal had cast an enormous shadow.

Whoosh! Another bat swooped by. It came so close, Josh felt its wing touch his hair.

"Aaaahhh! Get away!" shouted Josh.

Soon, dozens of bats poured from the hole in the ballroom's ceiling and started flying around the room. Josh crouched down and shielded his head with his arms.

The creatures circled the large room. Then, one by one, they flew through a jagged crack in one of the windows and out into the night. As suddenly as the bats had appeared, they were gone.

As Josh started to slowly stand up, he looked at the glass

doors and spotted Reggie behind them. The old man shuffled past the room, glaring at Josh.

Josh took a deep breath and glanced around to make sure there were no bats left. Then he dashed out of the ballroom.

Josh stood in the lobby, still shaky from what had just happened. He didn't want to bump into the grumpy old bellhop, so he decided to do some exploring upstairs.

As he climbed the wide staircase, Josh ducked to avoid a giant cobweb that hung like a curtain across the stairwell. The shriveled remains of flies and moths hung **preserved** among the web's sticky strands.

Josh reached the second floor and found himself in a long hallway with doors on either side. He set off along the corridor, counting the numbers on the doors: 201, 202 . . . 203, 204. Every few feet, a small, round light stuck out of the ceiling. Some of the lights glowed dimly, while others were burned out.

As he walked, Josh began to have a creepy feeling that he wasn't alone. Suddenly, one of the doors swung open and Reggie appeared from inside the room.

"What are *you* doing up here?" the bellhop asked angrily.

"I'm just looking around," said Josh nervously.

"There's nothing to see here," snarled Reggie. "Time for you to get back downstairs."

Reluctantly, Josh headed back the way he'd come. After a few steps, he turned to see if Reggie was watching him, but the bellhop was nowhere to be seen.

Room 213

The next morning, Josh set off to find his dad and help him with repairs in the old hotel. As Josh entered the lobby, he could hear raised voices coming from upstairs.

He walked up to the second floor and saw Dad and Reggie in the corridor where Josh had bumped into the old man the night before.

"Reggie, I have to check every room for possible repairs," said Dad, sounding **exasperated**. "I need the key for room 213."

"I said, there's no key for that room," answered Reggie. "No one ever goes in there."

"Fine, then I'll just **dismantle** the lock," said Dad.

Josh's dad dug around in his tool bag and took out a power drill. In a matter of seconds, he drilled through the lock. The door to room 213 creaked open, and Dad and Josh stepped inside.

The wall facing the door was covered with a huge brownish-red stain.

"Is that blood?" whispered Josh to his dad.

From behind them, Reggie said, "You shouldn't be in here."

"What happened?" gasped Dad.

Reggie looked around anxiously. "A long time ago . . . somebody . . . was murdered here," he said.

"That's horrible! Who was murdered?" Dad asked.

"A gangster named Johnny "Knuckles" Green . . . He was shot right there." Reggie pointed to the wall.

"Why didn't anyone clean up the blood?" asked Josh.

"The wall has been washed many times," said Reggie. "But the stain always comes back."

"Well, I have to do something to clean this up," said Dad, still appearing shocked as he left the room.

"You'd better get out of here, too, kid," Reggie warned Josh.

"I'm gonna stay," said Josh. "I want to help my dad."

Reggie hesitated. "Don't say I didn't warn you," he mumbled as he walked out of the room and closed the door behind him.

Josh looked around. He couldn't believe he was in a room where a real-life gangster was killed. He walked closer to the far wall to examine the bloodstain.

That's when he heard a **gravelly** voice.

"You need to take a walk, kid," the voice said. "Or else you'll be leaving this joint in the meat wagon."

Josh froze. Trembling, he slowly turned around. To his surprise, he was all alone!

Josh ran to the closed door and desperately tugged on it, but it was stuck. He kept yanking on the door until it suddenly flew open. Dad was on the other side holding cleaning supplies.

Josh started to wonder if maybe he'd imagined the **sinister** voice, so he didn't mention it to his dad. The two started working, and soon, Dad and Josh had scrubbed the wall clean.

"Nice job, kiddo. That bloodstain is gone for good," said Dad.

CHAPTER 3

The Gangster

After supper, Dad dozed in front of the television. Josh wasn't able to concentrate on the show, though. He kept thinking about the **menacing** voice in room 213. Eventually, Josh couldn't ignore his curiosity any longer. He crept out of the apartment. When he reached the doorway to the lobby, Josh heard Reggie's voice.

"That pesky repairman and his kid . . . interfering and poking around . . . I've been looking for seventy years."

Josh hid in the shadows and watched as Reggie pulled something from his pants pocket. It was a key to room 213!

Reggie stared **morosely** at the key. "I won't be needing this anymore," he mumbled. "Now that the repairman destroyed the lock."

Josh was shocked. Reggie had the key all along. So why had the old man told Dad there was no key? Now Josh was even more curious to find out what was going on in the mysterious room.

Once Reggie turned his back, Josh silently crept through the lobby and up the wide staircase. When he reached room 213, he hesitated for a moment. Then he pushed open the door, stepped inside, and switched on the light.

The dull bulb flickered to life. Josh couldn't believe what he saw. The huge bloodstain on the wall had reappeared!

Josh instantly felt sick to his stomach. Before he could decide what to do next, the door slammed shut behind him. Just as Josh reached for the doorknob, he heard the threatening voice.

"Didn't get the message, eh, kid?"

Josh turned. This time he was not alone.

In the dim light, Josh could just make out the shape of a man. He wore a dark suit and shiny black-and-white shoes. To Josh's horror, the man had a bloody, gaping hole in the middle of his body!

"Another one who thinks he's gonna get his hands on what's mine," the man growled.

Josh pressed his back against the door. As hard as he tried, he couldn't tear his eyes away from the **gory** wound.

The man threw back his head and **cackled**. "Yeah . . . take a good look. Even a bellyful of lead couldn't keep me from what's mine."

The man moved closer and reached inside his jacket . . .

"No one's gonna take it from me. Now get ready for the big sleep, kid!" he hissed.

"Help!" Josh screamed. Then he turned and pulled as hard as he could on the door. To Josh's relief, the door opened immediately, and he dashed downstairs.

As he ran, questions raced through Josh's mind. Had he just encountered the ghost of the murdered gangster, Johnny "Knuckles" Green? And what was the gangster trying to protect in room 213?

That night, Josh barely slept. By morning, he decided to find out more about what had happened in room 213. While his dad was out working on repairs, Josh stayed in the apartment and searched on his laptop.

He soon found a website about the Retreat Hotel's long history. One of the grainy photographs on the site showed a man dressed in a fancy suit. Beside him was a young bellhop holding two bags. The boy looked strangely familiar.

The photograph's caption read: *July 1939: The Retreat Hotel welcomes New York businessman Johnny Green.*

Josh kept searching and soon found an old newspaper article from the same year.

Murder at the Retreat Hotel

Gangster Johnny "Knuckles" Green was shot and killed yesterday by his rival, Frank "the Noose" Zeppo, at the Retreat Hotel. According to police, Zeppo was seeking revenge after Green stole one million dollars in cash

and jewels from him. Police have arrested Zeppo. The whereabouts of the stolen goods is currently unknown. The only witness to the murder was a 12-year-old bellhop, who survived the gunfire by hiding under a bed.

A photo alongside the story showed a blood-splattered wall and a **corpse** covered with a white sheet. Josh could make out a room number on the door—213.

As Josh stared at the photo of the murder scene, the ghostly gangster's angry words flickered through his mind:

"*A bellyful of lead couldn't keep me from what's mine . . . No one's gonna take it from me.*"

Josh wondered, could the stolen cash and jewels be hidden somewhere in the room?

CHAPTER 4

The Loot

Josh decided he had to find his dad and tell him what he'd discovered. He hurried through the lobby and up the stairs to the second floor, shouting, "Dad? Dad? Where are you?"

He heard a reply. "Josh, I'm in 213."

Josh rushed into the room. Dad was standing on top of a ladder in front of a wall covered with wooden panels.

"Josh, can you believe it?" Dad said. "That stain is back. The cleaning products didn't work. I'm going to have to paint over it, but first I need to fix these rotted wooden panels."

As Josh watched, his father used a screwdriver to pry a panel from the wall.

"Wait, what's this hole in the plaster?" said Dad. "There's something here."

Dad reached his hand far into the hole in the wall and pulled out an old, dusty bag.

Just then, to Josh's horror, the menacing shape of the murdered gangster **materialized**.

"Get your hands off my dough!" hissed the ghostly creature

as he pushed the ladder.

"Dad!" screamed Josh.

Josh watched as the ladder wobbled. His dad let go of the bag as he desperately tried to reach for the ladder.

The bag somersaulted through the air, showering the room with money and jewels. Dad fell backward onto the floor, and the ladder landed on top of him.

The gangster stood over Dad, blood dripping from the gunshot wound that had killed him years ago.

Dad groaned, and Josh rushed to push the ladder off of him.

As Dad shakily got to his feet, he saw the threatening **apparition** and his eyes grew wider. "What *is* that?" he shouted.

"What's going on?" The old bellhop shuffled into the room. Reggie noticed the money and gemstones strewn across the floor, and Josh saw a faint smile appear on his face. Then Reggie saw the gangster, and the smile disappeared.

"Come on!" said Reggie. "We need to get out of here."

"That's right, take a walk," snarled the angry ghost.

Josh, Dad, and Reggie hurried from the room, and Reggie slammed the door behind them. "I warned you not to go in there!" he yelled.

"What just happened?" asked Dad, looking utterly **bemused**.

"Dad, that was the ghost of Johnny Green," Josh hurriedly explained. "I think he's been haunting this room since he was murdered. He hid stolen money and jewels in the room!"

Josh suddenly remembered the photo of the young bellhop who had witnessed the murder.

"Wait . . . you were there when it happened weren't you, Reggie?" Josh asked the old man. "You were the bellhop who hid under the bed."

Reggie's face twitched nervously. Then his shoulders slumped and a look of **misery** passed over his wrinkled face.

"I saw it all," admitted Reggie. "The day Johnny Green got here, I peeked inside the bag and saw that it was filled with cash and jewels."

"That night, I brought Johnny a telephone message," continued Reggie. "Zeppo burst into the room, and they started arguing. Johnny told him he'd never get his hands on the bag of loot. When Zeppo raised his gun, I dove under the bed . . . then *bang!*"

"So, you've been looking for the bag all these years?" gasped Josh.

Reggie nodded. "For seventy years, I've stayed at this miserable place looking for it. I deserve to find it!"

Dad still looked confused. "You're telling me I just saw a ghost?" he asked Reggie.

Slowly, Reggie said, "Yes, that creature has **tormented** me for years. Every time I searched the room, it would chase me off."

Josh asked excitedly, "What are we going to do with the money, Dad?"

"Well, we're *not* going back into that room," said Dad. "I'm calling the hotel owners and the police. The cops will decide what to do with the stolen goods."

Josh glanced at Reggie. The old man looked tense and his eyes darted back and forth.

"Come on," said Dad. "I left my phone downstairs."

As Dad and Josh headed to their apartment, Reggie went back to the lobby.

After Dad called the police, he and Josh went into the lobby to wait for them.

"Where's Reggie?" said Dad. The old bellhop was not at the front desk, and the lobby was eerily quiet.

Dad and Josh both had the same thought at the same time: *Had Reggie returned to room 213?*

Josh and his dad raced up the stairs. When they reached the room, they saw the door was wide open. Cautiously, they peered inside.

The money and jewels were gone. A piece of paper lay on the floor. Josh picked it up and read:

The loot is mine now. Thanks for finding it. —R.

"I don't believe it," said Dad. "That **crafty** old devil came back up here and took off with everything!"

That's when Josh noticed something else. "Dad, look," he said. "The bloodstain is gone!"

The wall that had been splattered with Johnny Green's blood was now clean.

Then Josh looked down. Leading away from the wall was a trail of large, bloody footprints. The prints led to the room's door, then stopped—as if the wearer of the shoes had simply stepped out of the room and disappeared.

Josh looked back at the wall and then at the footprints.

"Dad . . . Reggie may have the loot," he said, "but I think he might also have a gangster on his tail!"

The Deadly Secret of Room 213

1. Why is Reggie unhappy that Josh and his dad have come to live at the hotel?

2. What encounters does Josh have with animals in the hotel?

3. What is happening in this scene?

4. At the end of the story, why does Josh think Johnny Green's ghost may be following Reggie?

5. Do you think it was wrong of Reggie to take the money and jewels, or did he deserve to have the loot? Explain your thoughts.

GLOSSARY

antique (an-TEEK) an object that is valuable because of its age and beauty

apparition (*ap*-uh-RISH-uhn) a ghost or ghostlike image

bellhop (BEL-hop) a person who works in a hotel carrying luggage and helping guests

bemused (bih-MYOOZD) puzzled or confused

cackled (KAK-uhld) laughed noisily

corpse (KORPS) a dead body

crafty (KRAF-tee) clever

dilapidated (dih-LAP-ih-day-tid) fallen into ruin

dismantle (dis-MAN-tuhl) to take apart

etched (ECHD) cut or carved into something

exasperated (eg-ZASS-puh-ray-tid) very annnoyed

gory (GORE-ee) covered in blood

gravelly (GRAV-uhl-ee) rough sounding

materialized (*muh*-TEER-ee-uh-lyzed) appeared in bodily form

menacing (MEN-ihs-ing) causing fear

misery (MIH-zuh-ree) great unhappiness

morosely (muh-ROHS-lee) gloomily

ornate (ore-NAYT) richly decorated

preserved (prih-ZURVD) kept in good condition

sinister (SIN-uh-stur) seeming evil and threatening

tormented (tore-MEN-tid) caused severe physical or mental suffering

ABOUT THE AUTHOR

Dee Phillips develops and writes nonfiction books for young readers and fiction books—including historical fiction—for middle graders and young adults. She loves to read and write stories that have a twist or an unexpected, thought-provoking ending. Dee lives near the ocean on the southwest coast of England. A keen hiker, her biggest ambition is to one day walk the entire coast of Great Britain.

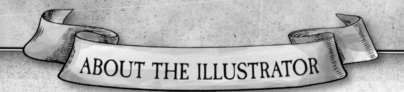

ABOUT THE ILLUSTRATOR

Anthony Resto graduated from the American Academy of Art with a BFA in Watercolor. He has been illustrating children's books, novellas, and comics for six years, and is currently writing his own children's book. His most recent illustrated books include *Happyland: A Tale in Two Parts* and *Oracle of the Flying Badger*. You can find his other illustrated books and fine art works at anthonyresto.com. In his free time, he enjoys restoring his vintage RV and preparing for the zombie apocalypse.